WITHDRAWN

CRAZY WANDA

CRAZY WANDA

An Angela Constantine Novella

TERRY GOODKIND

CHAPTER ONE

Just as Angela was locking her pickup before going in to her bartending job at Barry's Place, trouble rolled up on a rickety, pink girl's bicycle. Under the harsh glare of the light on the power pole at the edge of the lot, the frayed bill of the man's leather baseball cap cast a shadow down over his gaunt face. His tattered white undershirt had tea-colored stains. The way his lips sank in around an unfiltered cigarette betrayed the fact that he was all gums. By his rattling cough as he had coasted to a stop, Angela was pretty sure that he either had lung cancer or was well on his way to getting it.

The old man spread his legs and planted his feet on the ground to steady the bike as he cleared phlegm from his throat. He leaned to the side to spit out a big wad. At least he spit away from her.

His gaze drifted up from her knee-high boots, up her bare, long legs and cutoff shorts, finally reaching her face. He squinted his left eye against a rising curl of smoke as he took a drag from the cigarette between his sunken lips. The glow from that long drag momentarily lit the coarse stubble covering the contours and folds of his leathery skin.

He took the cigarette from his mouth with the first two fingers of his left hand and flicked off the ash.

"Well, well, well," he drawled in a raspy voice that still possessed the hint of a once-tough man. "Didn't you grow up to be as pretty as an angel."

Angela was scowling. She had seen him panhandling in the parking lot before, but this was the first time he had ever approached her.

1

She'd parked with her front bumper almost touching the wall of the bar. He was straddling his bike at the end of the gap between her truck and the car in the next spot.

Without a word, she started to go past him. He put a hand out to lean against the side of her truck and block her path. It looked to her like the practiced reflex of a man who had used that same move to stop countless young women.

"Get out of my way," she said with menace.

He gestured beseechingly with the hand holding the cigarette. "Might you give an old friend a bit of help?"

"We aren't 'old friends,'" she said.

She knew what "help" drunks and crackheads usually wanted. She had no intention of giving him any of her money. She worked hard and didn't want what she earned going up in smoke.

"Oh, but we are," he said, squinting at her with the one eye without smoke in it. "I'm Albert. I'm your father."

Angela was caught off guard for only an instant. She huffed a laugh. "Yeah, right. I don't know an Albert."

"I was a friend of your mother, Sally."

"So were lots of guys."

Any one of the drunks, tweakers, or dealers who hung around their trailer could have been her father. It wasn't like it would have been a rare conquest. Neither her mother nor the degenerates she slept with gave paternity much thought.

Over the years Angela saw all those men up close, many without their clothes. To Angela it didn't matter which one of them had fathered her. They were all psychos. She didn't remember Albert hanging around the trailer when she was little, but then, it was hard to remember all the creeps she'd seen back then.

Since she had no intention of giving this man any money, talking to him would be pointless. She needed to get inside for her shift. As she went to push past him, he rolled his bicycle forward, planting the front wheel against the truck's back fender to pen her in.

"I just need some money to help me get by. Can't you see your way to giving your poor old dad a twenty?"

Much to his helpless annoyance, Angela grabbed the bike's head tube, lifted the front end, and set it aside.

That was when he pulled a knife. "You look like you could easily spare a twenty for your needy father," he said with a cunning grin. Even though it was a relatively small knife and in poor condition, it was easily big enough to be lethal. "But since you want to be such a heartless little bitch about it, I'll take all you got."

Because she was conceived by addicts and had spent nine months developing in a womb awash with alcohol and every kind of illicit drug her mother could get her hands on, it was something of a miracle that Angela had been born at all. While she might have appeared normal, she knew that she had been born broken, left with the quite abnormal and freaky ability to recognize killers by their eyes.

She knew by this man's eyes that he was in the declining stages of dangerous, but he wasn't a killer.

Of course, that didn't mean, even at this late stage of his life, that he couldn't start a new profession. She could tell by his eyes and his hair-trigger temperament that he had been an intimidating man most people would have avoided. Now, though, he was just a shell of his former self, a lion without his teeth.

"Quit stalling. Do as I say and hand over all your money. I'd hate to have to stab my own daughter."

"If you really were Sally's friend, then you would know that neither my mother nor the degenerates she slept with had any idea who fathered me, so your claim is baseless."

"Well, I slept with her a time or two, so it could just as well be me."

He waved the knife in her direction, hoping it would urge her to hand over her money.

"Get that knife out of my face and get out of my way or I'll call the police and file assault charges against you. I'd bet you have a long rap sheet and outstanding warrants, so they would be happy to throw you in jail."

He grew the kind of calculating smile that Angela knew all too well from men who intended her harm, even if they didn't intend murder.

The once-dangerous man reemerged in his tone. "One way or another you're going to give me your money."

She leaned down toward him, close enough to smell his stink. "Move."

When he thrust the knife toward her she was ready. She caught his wrist and turned his frail arm out to the side, away from her. The ravages of a life of drugs and alcohol had left him skin and bones, hardly a worthy adversary for her strength.

Yipping in pain, and apparently still intent on stabbing her, he struggled to wrestle his arm away. She held his wrist in a viselike grip as she kept his arm twisted aside. With her other hand she pried his little finger and then his ring finger from the handle of the knife, bending both back until he twisted and howled in pain.

Once she had extinguished his aggression with a good bit of pain, she released his fingers, grabbed the end of the handle, and twisted the knife out of his hand.

"Give it back!" he cried, cradling his sore fingers with his other hand. "It's mine! Give it back!"

He reminded her of nothing so much as a shriveled, gnomelike character whining for his magic knife back, as if it were the source of his strength.

She pointed the tarnished blade at his face. "Get lost. If you ever threaten me again you had better hope that the cops take you to jail to protect you from me."

His gaze went to the large tattoo across her throat. "I see now what kind of angel you really are."

"Then I guess you had best get on down the road."

Angela heaved the knife away. It skittered across the parking lot and came to rest in weeds growing in the cracked asphalt at the edge of the road.

He glanced her way briefly to see if she intended to hit him, then pedaled away, intent on retrieving his knife. The bike wobbled as he tried to control it with one hand on one handlebar and a wrist on the other.

Angela felt a little bad about hurting such a frail old man, but she had a rule: Don't be nice to people who try to kill you.

CHAPTER 2

Angela woke with a start from a dead sleep when she heard a hollow thud come from outside the house. She snatched her gun off the nightstand before her feet had even hit the floor. A rush of adrenaline flashed like ice through her veins and brought her wide awake in an instant.

Her heart hammered as she sat on the edge of the bed for a moment, listening intently, trying to make sense of the sound, trying to think of what it could be. It had been too loud to be a pinecone hitting the ground or even the roof. Those often made a thud, but not this loud. This had been something more substantial—a quick crack of sound that had reverberated back from the woods.

She wondered briefly if it could be dear old Dad, but the old derelict couldn't possibly have pedaled his pink girl's bicycle this far out of town. He would have died of exhaustion before he got very far from his haunts.

Unless someone had given him a ride.

Ducking low as she crossed the room, she darted a glance out the bedroom door, first to the left toward the front, and then to the right toward the back door, where she thought the sound had come from. She knew that just because the sound had come from out back didn't mean someone couldn't be out front as well, or even inside the house. Living alone and with her house being so isolated, Angela always worried about a home invasion.

Her long drive had a stout cable across it, but that wouldn't stop a big wire cutter. The security provided by the cable was more in the statement it made, along with a skull and crossbones sign warning against trespassing. The only purpose in cutting the cable, though, would be to drive up the long drive to the house. She hadn't heard car tires crunching on gravel.

Just to be sure, she cleared the kitchen and then the living room on the way through. When she was away from home she carried a Walther P22, because it was lighter and much easier to conceal, but it required exceptional accuracy. If the shot placement was on target, though, it was as deadly as any gun but without overpenetration or making a huge, bloody mess. That was why it was the choice of assassins.

In her house when it was dark she would likely only be able to see a bad guy's dark shape. For that reason, she kept a Glock 9 mm loaded with hollow-points on her nightstand. It only needed to hit center mass to stop a threat.

Stepping silently across the living room in her bare feet, Angela peeked out past the edge of the curtain to check the yard. The moonlight provided enough light to see that there was no car in sight, only her primer-gray pickup.

After the quick appraisal out the front, gun up and at the ready, Angela hurried to the back door between the bedroom and the kitchen. She scanned out the small window in the door. The dense forest of towering pines blocked much of the moonlight, but because she'd been asleep her eyes were well adjusted to the dark.

She spotted two shapes moving through those shadows. They were too low to be deer. She thought at first that they were dogs.

Then, when one of them moved into the moonlight between the shadows, she saw that it was a dark-colored wolf. More than that, it was a wolf she recognized.

It was Bardolph.

Bardolph had been shot by a sheriff's deputy the previous winter. Angela had been angry that the deputy had shot the animal. She didn't want it to suffer a slow, agonizing death, and she didn't have the heart to kill it, so she had taken it to an animal emergency hospital. While it was there the staff who had cared for it had named it Bardolph.

Because the wolf was potentially quite dangerous, once it had recovered Angela released it quite a distance away from her house into the woods where she had found it. It had returned the favor by attacking a maniac who had tried to kill her. She had saved its life, and it had in turn saved hers. It had seemed that karma was alive and well in the universe.

She presumed the wolf would live in the vast preserve surrounding her home. Now it had shown up by her house. Since wolves avoided people, she didn't know why it would come around.

Angela opened the door to get a better look. It was a relatively warm summer night, so she stood in the doorway in only her underwear, watching. It was then that she spotted the second wolf. Bardolph stayed back by the trees as he watched the second wolf investigating the backyard. It was lighter-colored and a bit smaller. Angela was pretty sure it was female.

"Well, my old friend," she murmured, "it looks like you found yourself a mate."

Wanting to see, smell, and touch everything in the yard, the female rubbed against the picnic table, leaving her scent. Angela saw, then, that a board she'd left on the table had been knocked off onto a knob of rock sticking up from the ground. She realized that that had been the sound she had heard.

The whole time the she-wolf investigated the backyard, she kept a wary eye on Angela; then she abruptly advanced toward Angela, snarling, lips curled back, showing her teeth. It was a frightening sight.

Angela had her gun up and at the ready. She didn't want to shoot the creature, but she would if she had to. She hoped simply pointing the gun at the snarling beast would be enough to keep it at bay.

It wasn't.

The female wolf suddenly advanced aggressively toward Angela, mouth opened, teeth bared, closing the distance.

Just before Angela pulled the trigger, Bardolph loped up to intercept the female. He growled and snapped at her. In a display of dominance, he put his neck over hers and pushed her head down, as if to tell her to back off. She licked his face in submission and then they twined their necks together for a moment before bounding off into the woods.

Angela stood in the doorway, gun lowered to her side, watching the dark woods where the pair had vanished. It had been an amazing sight. She was thrilled to have seen him again.

She hadn't seen Bardolph for months, not since back in the dead of a bitter winter. For the life of her, Angela couldn't figure out why he had come around her place in the woods, and why he had brought his new mate.

She heard the pair, then, off on Grandfather Mountain, howl at the moon.

Her life in the woods, in the house her grandparents had built, was her sanctuary of solitude. It made up for the other part of her life working with her own messenger service and at Barry's Place tending bar. Those two lives—one in the woods and one in Milford Falls—could not be more different. While they seemed opposites, in some ways, when it came to the evil men who occasionally crossed paths with her, those two lives were connected. Those evil men ended their murderous careers in Angela's world of solitude, never to be seen again.

CHAPTER 3

As Angela set beers down in front of a boisterous group of men at a round table, one of them, Ricky Sparling, leaned back in his chair.

"Where's Wanda?"

Angela put a bowl of pretzels on the table as she flipped the tray around with her other hand and tucked it under her arm. "Beats me," she said over the loud thump of rock music. "She should have been here hours ago."

It was busy, even for a Friday night. With Wanda a no-show, Angela was being run ragged trying to keep up with orders. At least the extra tips helped soothe her annoyance at Wanda for leaving her high and dry.

The men were a lumber crew from one of the remaining small operations working just outside Milford Falls. Ricky Sparling owned the small company and it made him a good living. They specialized in select cutting from property owners. They all smelled of fresh-cut pine, gasoline, and smoke from diesel equipment.

Ricky had on a red plaid shirt with the sleeves rolled up. He leaned in on his elbows.

"I'm buying this round." He grinned at Angela as he handed her some folded bills. "Keep the change."

The men chuckled a little when he winked at her. She didn't respond to his wink. "When Wanda comes in I'll let her know you were asking after her."

Angela hurried back to the bar to get the next order ready. She set the tray on a stack at the side and noticed Barry on the phone in the hall. She quickly opened a bottle of beer for an older man sitting at the bar and scooped up the money he laid down. She rang the beer up on the cash register and gave the man his change.

With the loud rock music that always played in the bar, Angela couldn't hear what Barry was saying, although by his animated gestures she could tell he was miffed.

When the call ended he quickly ducked into the cooler where the kegs were kept and returned with a hand truck loaded with cases of bottled beer for the refrigeration unit behind the bar.

Angela gestured. "The second tap isn't working."

Barry's expression twisted with long-suffering displeasure as he loaded beer bottles into the cooler. "Probably that damn coupling again. I don't think I have a new one. I'll have to see if I can fix it after closing."

"Something wrong?" Angela asked.

"Crazy Wanda."

"Ah," she said with a knowing nod as she drew beers and poured shots for the next order. "So what's her excuse for being late?"

Barry straightened and leaned closer. "She got her ass thrown in jail."

Angela rolled her eyes. "Again?"

"Yeah."

"What's she done this time?"

"She says it's all a big misunderstanding."

Angela let out a half laugh. "Isn't it always?"

"She says she wanted to get her things from her ex-boyfriend's place, but he wouldn't ever meet her there to let her in. So, of course, crazy Wanda broke a window and let herself in. At least, that's her story."

Wanda could turn the most ordinary of situations into drama. It seemed she had now turned a simple breakup with her most recent boyfriend into an arrest. Wanda was a walking, talking soap opera.

Even though she was often late, Barry didn't fire her, because she was good at her job—when she was there—so on balance she was good for the bar. With her naturally friendly nature and bubbly personality, she got men to stick around and buy drinks they didn't know they wanted.

"Anyway," Barry said, "she asked me to please come bail her out."

"Why you? Let her parents bail her out."

"That's what I told her. She says they won't answer their phone."

Angela nodded knowingly. "Caller ID."

Barry frowned up at her from putting bottles in the cooler. "What?"

"They probably saw on their caller ID that it was a number from the jail and they didn't want to bail her out again."

Barry sighed as he went back to loading more bottles into the cooler. "That makes sense."

Angela didn't know anyone who got hauled to jail as often as Wanda did, and it was never for anything serious. It was always some trivial issue she managed to blow up into a fracas.

One time she got pulled over for running a stop sign. She argued with the cop and angrily refused to sign the ticket. She became increasingly belligerent until she had to be restrained. She spent the night in jail until she saw the judge in the morning. He dropped the charges in return for her paying a big fine for the ticket.

As a result of missing work while sitting in jail, she got behind in her bills. Bill collectors started harassing her, which set her off in fits of anger when she stormed into work.

"It's your own damn fault," Angela had told her when she was complaining about all her troubles.

"It's not my fault!" Wanda protested.

Angela quietly reminded her that had she simply signed the ticket, she would have paid a less expensive fine and not missed work and then she wouldn't have gotten behind in her bills and bill collectors wouldn't be after her. It was so inarguable, and put to her in such a calm manner, that it had stopped Wanda's fit cold. After a moment of grumbling, Wanda had finally said, "I suppose you're right."

Angela somehow ended up being the one person in Wanda's life she would listen to. Angela assumed it was because she didn't really care if Wanda listened to her or not, while everyone else did and they almost always shouted at her, argued with her, or lectured her. While most people could set her off with one wrong word, Angela's dispassionate advice had the opposite effect on her.

Over time Wanda came to consider Angela a trusted friend. As far as Angela could tell, her only friend. Wanda would confide things to Angela that she would confide to no one else. Angela wasn't trying to befriend Wanda or win her over, she was simply treating her the way she treated everyone.

Although Wanda considered her a trusted friend, Angela most certainly didn't feel the same about Wanda. Angela didn't have friends and didn't want any.

She did feel a bit sorry for her, though. She was a scatterbrain without common sense who acted before she thought.

Wanda had big breasts and a big mouth to match. She also had an open, friendly nature that made her the life of any party. The male customers loved her flirty personality, as well as her big breasts. The women, not so much. Especially when she put an easygoing hand on their men. Wanda was only too happy to be the center of attention. That was why Barry put up with Wanda's troublesome side.

"I really can't leave the bar while we're open," Barry said. "I wish Wanda wouldn't pull this crap."

"You want me to go spring her?" she asked.

Angela always did her best to avoid authorities. Unlike Wanda, she didn't like to give the police any reason to take notice of her or remember her. But Barry was a good guy who had given her a chance with a good paying job and she felt bad that Wanda was dragging him into it.

"And be down the both of you?" He shook his head. "Besides, those legs of yours sell a lot more drinks than a pudgy guy in khaki pants."

Angela had to smile. "I suppose so. Why not let her stew until after closing?"

"That makes sense." He thought about it briefly. "But after closing I need to take care of that damn tap coupling, the receipts, stocking up, and then I need to tally everything."

"Why don't I go bail her out after closing?"

Barry considered momentarily. "Tomorrow is Saturday. It's going to be a busy night. Lots of men will be coming in tomorrow night and I really need her here." He gave Angela a sideways look. "If you wouldn't mind..."

"That's my other job, remember? I pick up packages." Angela smiled. "You get things ready for tomorrow and I'll go get the crazy lady."

CHAPTER 4

Angela found a parking spot on the street around the corner from the entrance to the police station. She hadn't wanted to walk into the station wearing the cutoff shorts she wore at work in the bar. Fortunately, she had a pair of jeans in her truck and was able to change first. Since it was spitting rain and threatening to turn into a downpour, she put on a lightweight, hooded, waterproof jacket that she always kept in her pickup.

The hood of the black jacket covered her red-tipped, platinum-blond hair. Like her cutoff shorts, her hair drew attention, which was all well and good in the bar, or out in public, or when luring in a killer, but not so desirable in a police station. With the jacket zipped all the way up, it also covered the big tattoo across her throat, which she would rather not show off in a police station because it was something people remembered.

With her hood up against the rain and the drawstring pulled tight, she looked reasonably unremarkable among the people in the station. Barry had already found out that Wanda had been arraigned on trespassing charges earlier in the day and was being held awaiting bail. At the arraignment her bond had been set at a thousand dollars, but only ten percent cash was required.

The police station was relatively busy, even in the middle of the night, or more likely, Angela realized, because it was the middle of the night. As she knew all too well from working in a bar, darkness seemed to bring trouble out of the woodwork.

Angela found the bond window, paid the bail, and signed some papers. While she was there she asked to read the charges. The policewoman behind the counter pulled a sheet out and handed it to Angela. When she finished reading it, she thanked the woman and handed it back.

The benches were already packed, so she leaned against the wall as she waited. As she waited, she appraised the eyes of people, especially men, making sure she was not in the presence of someone seriously dangerous.

It was a half hour before a female officer came out from a hallway with Wanda in tow. The policewoman took her to a counter where she was given back her big handbag and the contents for her to check.

As Angela watched Wanda put her loop earrings back on, she realized that while she thought of Wanda as one seriously screwed-up woman, she was actually quite striking. She was the kind of woman that men seemed to fall in love with far too quickly.

Her head was shaved partway up on each side, leaving her thick, black hair to stand up on top and tumble down her broad shoulders in back. Sometimes she put it into a single, fat braid. Angela wouldn't want that style of hair, but it worked well with the package that was Wanda.

She was wearing a pink tank top that had difficulty containing her breasts, a black miniskirt, and red strap heels. Apparently, she had been ready to go in to work at the bar when she had been arrested and taken to jail. Her figure was actually quite shapely, even if her outfit was over-the-top. Over-the-top worked just fine in her job at Barry's Place and made her good tips.

Wanda, jamming her things back into the big, gray leather handbag, looked like bottled fury as Angela stepped up to the counter beside her. "Thanks for coming," Wanda grumbled with a quick sideways glance. "I didn't want to bother you. I asked Barry to come. Why didn't he come?" It was more an angry indictment than a question.

"Yeah, well, Barry was pretty busy trying to fix a broken tap and getting everything else ready for a busy Saturday night, so I offered to come get you."

She nodded to Angela as she cast a glare back at the disinterested police behind the counter. "Let's get out of this dump."

"I'm parked just around the corner," Angela said as they walked out into the light rain.

Wanda folded her arms against the wet night chill and put her head down against the steady, light rain. She hurried as best she could in high heels.

Angela unlocked her truck and let Wanda in first to get her out of the rain, then took off the jacket and slipped in behind the wheel. Once the truck was started she turned on the heater.

"I left my car in the alley behind Brad's place. I was getting my stuff when he came home and called the cops." She looked over. "Want to stop somewhere and get a drink? I could use a good stiff drink. I know a place—"

"Thanks, but no thanks. It's been a long day. I'll take you to get your car, then we both need to get home and get a good night's sleep." Angela glanced over as Wanda looked out the side window into the dark night. "Tomorrow night is going to be busy."

Wanda turned back. "Was it busy tonight?"

"As a matter of fact, it was. Without you there to help I feel like I ran a marathon."

Wanda stared out again at the lights flashing past in the rain. Her bluster was already fading. "Sorry to leave you hanging."

"Ricky Sparling asked about you. I told him that I would pass the message along to you."

Wanda suddenly looked concerned. "You didn't tell him I was in jail, did you?"

"It was before you called Barry. I told him all I knew, that you were late, and I didn't know where you were."

Wanda let out a sigh of relief. She fished her phone out of her handbag and checked her messages, then started writing a text. Angela looked out of the corner of her eye and could see that it was to Ricky. It said something about making it up to him.

Ricky wasn't the sharpest axe in the woods, but he worked hard and made good money. He also had the kind of weak-willed personality that needed a strong woman to give him directions. Wanda was just that sort of woman and more.

After she sent the text she put the phone away and turned to Angela. "Say, would you mind if I spent the night at your place?"

Angela nearly drove off the road. She quickly pulled herself together. "You need to go home to your own place."

"Well, I gave up my apartment to live with Brad. Since he kicked me out so he could screw around with some whore, my place at the moment is back home with my God-fearing parents. If I go there I'll have to listen to another lecture about God's plan for me and how I'm disrespecting him. They're such jerks."

Wanda was gasoline. Her parents seemed to be a lit match.

She smoothed her skirt on her lap. "So, what do you say? Can I crash with you?"

Angela thought that being simple and straightforward would be best. "Sorry, no."

Wanda frowned. "Why not?"

"First of all, nothing personal, but I never let anyone stay at my house. I work long, hard hours. It's my sanctuary away from everything and everyone and I want it to stay that way. Secondly, I have no intention of making the situation more comfortable for you just because you screwed up."

Wanda looked out the side window again. "Yeah, I guess I did kind of screw things up."

"You have keys to your mom and dad's house, right?"

Wanda nodded.

"And you still have your room there, right?"

"Yeah. They keep it for me. I think they're hoping I'll somehow magically turn back to being fourteen so they can have a do-over with raising me."

"So, listen to me. I want you to go home, quietly let yourself in, leave a note on their coffeemaker saying you're asleep in your room and to let you sleep in because you got in late and you have to work Saturday night. Draw a heart on it, or something. Can you do that?"

"I suppose," she mumbled. "But it wasn't my fault—"

"So your ex-boyfriend broke his own window and called the cops and made up a story that it was you?" Angela wasn't going to let her shift the blame for her situation.

"Well, no. But if he wouldn't have—"

"When I paid the bond, I read Brad's statement in the complaint to the police."

"Yeah, well Brad is a lying asshole." Wanda thought about that a moment and then was overcome with a curious frown. "Where do you live, anyway? I never have heard where you live."

Angela never let anyone know where she lived. She greatly valued her privacy—and other things about her place in the woods. Her mail even went to Mike's Mail Service.

"I live alone out in the country in a place my grandfather built."

"Doesn't that get kind of lonely?"

"No. I don't get lonely. I guess I'm strange that way." Angela knew Wanda was trying to change the subject of her guilt. She didn't let her. "So did you steal Brad's gun?"

Wanda looked over in surprise. "What?"

"Brad said in his statement to the police that you stole his gun."

"Brad's an asshole. I told you that."

"Did you steal his gun?"

Wanda huffed. "Brad's got this big three-fifty-seven Magnum revolver. He likes to show it off because he thinks it makes his dick bigger."

"Did you steal it?"

"What would I want with a gun? He changed the locks and wouldn't meet me there to get my stuff, so before I came in to work I broke a little window and went in to get my clothes. Big deal; it's just ten dollars' worth of glass to fix the window. He's just trying to cause trouble for me because I caught him cheating."

"Did you steal his gun?"

"He held me against my will for the police." She leaned over indignantly. "That's kidnapping! He threatened me. He said if I tried to leave he'd hurt me. Brad has a nasty temper. He's smacked me around a few times, so I knew he wasn't bluffing.

"Then these hard-ass cops showed up. After they cuffed me and patted me down real good, if you know what I mean, they put me in the back of their police car while they searched my car looking for the gun Brad told them I stole.

"The only thing in my car was my clothes that I took out of Brad's place. They didn't find any gun or anything else of his. That's why they couldn't charge me with theft of a weapon. Brad's an asshole and he was just trying to cause me trouble."

"You're lucky the charge was only trespassing."

"The police only took me to jail because Brad insisted on pressing charges, and trespassing was all they could come up with. I didn't take anything other than my own clothes, so they couldn't charge me with theft. If the cops wouldn't have been such pricks they would have just let me go and told me to stay away from Brad's place or they would arrest me if I came back. That's what they should have done. But they didn't. They wanted me in the back of their car with my hands cuffed behind my back, so they could watch me in the backseat and try to look up my skirt." She stared ahead. "Perverts."

Angela drove in silence, wondering if there was a grain of truth in Wanda's story. She knew from personal experience that there were police who could be real jerks. There were times when they came to her mother's trailer when they had been more than jerks. That's why she didn't like having anything to do with them. She gritted her teeth at her own memories of encounters with police on a power trip.

Wanda used her fingers to fluff her wet hair. "Did Ricky say he thinks I'm hot?"

Angela came back from her unpleasant memories and frowned over at Wanda. "What is this, study hall in high school?"

Wanda shrugged. "I think I'm falling in love with him." She frowned as a sudden thought came to her. She leaned a little toward Angela. "Ricky Sparling is mine. Don't you dare wrap those long legs of yours around him."

Angela kept her gaze out at the rainy road. "Ricky Sparling is married."

"I know that. But his wife is a bitch. She cheats on him."

"Isn't that what he's doing with you?"

"Yeah, but that's because the bitch won't give him a divorce because she wants his money, so he's going to have to divorce her instead. But first he needs to hire a private detective to follow her around and get proof of all her extramarital affairs so he has grounds for the divorce. I can't imagine why any woman would do that to him. I'd never cheat on him. He'd be all I ever wanted."

Angela was tired. She knew Wanda's fuse was already lit, so she kept her thoughts to herself as she drove to Brad's run-down little house in a run-down part of town. Even this late, and even in the rain, there were people out on the street or huddled against buildings. From a lifetime of experience, she could easily spot half a dozen drug deals going down.

She always carried a gun, if not on her, then in the center armrest, so she wasn't worried, but this wasn't a neighborhood where women should be alone. She drove into the alley behind Brad's house and stopped behind Wanda's faded red hatchback.

"Go home and get some sleep," she told Wanda. "I need you there tomorrow night. If you don't pull it together Barry is going to finally get fed up and fire you."

Wanda nodded. "Yeah, I know. I'll be there. Thanks for coming and getting me, Angela."

Halfway out of the truck, she stopped and turned back. "Can I ask you a question?"

"You're just full of questions tonight."

Wanda grinned. "I'm a curious girl. What does that big tattoo across your throat mean? 'Dark Angel.' What's it mean?"

"Your parents taught you to pray, didn't they?"

"Are you kidding? I spent half my childhood on my knees praying."

"Then pray that you never have a reason to learn what it means. Good night, Wanda."

Wanda wasn't sure what Angela meant. "All right. Good night. And thanks again for bailing me out. You're a doll."

Angela waited until Wanda had started her car and driven off down the alley before backing out into the street and turning around to go home.

She was glad to be rid of the crazy lady so she could finally go home to peace and quiet and get some sleep.

Home. It suddenly occurred to her why Bardolph the wolf had come around her house with his new mate.

"I'll be damned," she said under her breath as she drove through the rainy night toward her remote house in the mountains where wolves lived.

CHAPTER 5

Wanda drove her small Chevy hatchback slowly down the narrow alley, navigating around tipped-over trash cans and junk appliances people had piled to the side. She watched in her rearview mirror, through the rain running down the back window, as Angela backed her truck out of the alley, swung around, and headed off in the opposite direction. As soon as the lights of Angela's pickup were out of sight, Wanda turned right out of the alley and drove around the block to come back in the alley again.

Angela was the one person Wanda trusted. Angela wasn't like anyone else she knew. She was smarter than anyone else she knew. Not necessarily book smart, but life smart. It often felt like Angela could look into her eyes and tell what she was thinking, or even what she had done. Angela just seemed to know things right out of thin air. Angela always told Wanda the truth, but without bitching at her like everyone else. Wanda adored her like a big sister.

Even so, Wanda could hardly tell Angela everything.

She drove slowly, hoping not to make enough noise to wake anyone. She stopped in the same spot she'd just been parked in. She left the engine running and the headlights on. She got out and pushed the door closed without latching it so as to make as little noise as possible.

She looked across the alley at Brad's house. The lights weren't on. She would have loved to have thrown a rock through his bedroom window. It would probably scare the crap out of whatever whore he was sleeping with.

But she had more important things to do.

She squatted down in the weeds beside three heavily dented trash cans. In the light from the headlights, she looked behind the cans, among scrap pieces of boards and old wood paneling. She found the small square of weathered plywood she was looking for. Its edges were delaminated, wrinkled, and cracking apart. Afraid of getting splinters, she lifted it carefully. With all the spiderwebs in the weeds, she was worried about spiders.

There, under the pieces of plywood, was the zippered cloth gun case holding the .357 Magnum revolver and three full boxes of bullets. She reached in and quickly pulled it out, hoping not to give any spiders time to bite her.

Once she had retrieved the gun, she hurried back to her car and put the gun case into the big, gray, sloppy handbag she was carrying that day expressly because it was big enough to easily conceal the gun. She smiled to herself as she put the car in gear and rolled slowly out of the alley.

She had to smile, too, at having the forethought to hide the gun. She hadn't known Brad would come home and catch her, much less call the police, but she had been concerned that he might see her and follow her, or even, once he came home and found his gun missing, go to her parents and break into her car looking for it. She'd hidden it so she could come back at a later date and retrieve it after things had cooled down.

Since the police had already searched her car, that had convinced Brad, and the police, that she hadn't taken his gun.

She was smarter than both Brad and the cops. She'd told them when they cuffed her that it was a bad neighborhood. Anyone could have gotten in his house and stolen it. She'd even convinced Angela that she hadn't taken Brad's gun.

She had to grin at the thought of police searching her car and failing to find the gun Brad had been yelling about, and at the look on Brad's face when they came back and told him she didn't have his gun. He'd been so sure she had taken it. It made him look stupid.

Brad had told her once, when he was showing off the handgun, that a hollow-point .357 slug would go into a person like a nickel and come out the other side like a bag of quarters.

He thought the gun made him tough. She wondered how tough he felt now. At first, she hadn't really cared about the gun, she just wanted to take it away from him. Now, she was glad to have it. The gun made her just as tough as he was.

Wanda's mood darkened as she drove through the alley, envisioning blowing Brad's brains out. It felt good thinking about it.

By the time she reached her parents' house she was exhausted from all the trouble Brad and the police had caused her. She wished she could somehow get even with him for cheating on her and throwing her out. She slipped her hand into her handbag and felt the gun case. She smiled at having taken the bastard's prize handgun. It felt like she had taken his manhood.

Wanda parked on the street in front of her parents' house behind a car up on blocks. She was careful never to leave any valuables in her car because it was such a bad neighborhood. Even though her car was a piece of shit, it was better than most of the cars in the neighborhood. She hated the place.

She had keys to the house, so she let herself in and then quietly closed the front door, hoping not to have to talk to her parents. When she turned around she was momentarily startled by the figure of her father standing in the shadows not far away at the bottom of the stairs.

She put a hand to the top of her chest, catching her breath. "You scared the crap out of me!"

His expression was grim. Standing there in her mother's fluffy slippers, plaid boxer shorts, and an undershirt he looked silly.

"I saw that you called from the police station," he said. "What have you done this time?"

Wanda's temper heated. "Why didn't you answer the damn phone and come help get me out?"

"Your whole life your mother and I have done our best to raise you to be a God-fearing young woman. When you got into trouble we prayed with you to drive the devil's influence from you and to guide you to the right path. But you always let the devil back in.

"I work too hard for my money to use it to bail you out of jail when it could go to better use at the church. I'll not steal from what should go to them to bail you out anymore. You don't need bail money, you need the devil beaten out of you. You're not too old for that, you know."

"Fuck you," she snapped as she stormed past.

Wanda had never walked the right path, as he put it. She had always pretended, but she never really cared about any of their religious nonsense. Once she had moved out, she thought she was finally free of it all, and now, because of that bastard Brad, here she was, right back in her parents' house again.

She slammed her bedroom door and then flopped down on the bed. She put her head in her hands. She was sick and tired of everyone causing her problems.

She wished that she hadn't given up her apartment, but Brad had wanted her to move in with him. She realized now that he had been playing her so he could have ready access to pussy.

She needed to get a place to stay, but bill collectors were already after her and her credit was shot. Apartments checked credit records. She dreaded the thought of having to get a slum apartment, but things would get ugly if she stayed at her parents' for long.

She fished her phone out of her big handbag.

sorry i missed u at the bar. my a hole x was causing me problems again.

In a few moments he texted back. *Sorry. I was asleep. You going to be at Barry's Place tonight?*

Yes.

Okay, I'll talk to you then. Good night, babe.

Wanda flicked the phone back on the bed. She was wired after confronting her father, as if he knew anything about life outside his stupid church. She had wanted to talk to Ricky. It irritated her that he would rather sleep than talk to her. She thought, then, that he probably couldn't talk because he was in bed right next to his wife.

Wanda was going to have to do something about that.

26

CHAPTER 6

After a busy day with her messenger service, delivering packets for her lawyer customers, Angela finally made her way up her long drive, glad to be home if only for a little while. She always loved the solitude of her place in the woods among the mountains. She was hungry and looked forward to making herself some dinner before changing for work at Barry's Place. The peace and quiet in the woods surrounding her house steeled her for the noise and all the people at the bar where she worked.

It was tough having two jobs, but for the time being the work was there and the money was good. She missed not being able to spend more time at home hiking through the mountains, but there might not always be work. Growing up as she had had taught her to expect that bad times would always come around.

She put olive oil in a pan on the stove and then laid in a chicken breast. She left the back door open so that the aroma of the cooking chicken would drift out into the woods while she went through the mail she had picked up from Mike's Mail Service on her way home. She threw away the advertisements and set the bills aside on the kitchen table.

When she leaned back to look out the open back door, she saw Bardolph not far away at the edge of the woods. He was pacing. Angela smiled at seeing him. As she had done every day for several weeks, she had taken two half chickens out of the refrigerator.

She picked up the chicken waiting on the counter and took it outside. Bardolph knew her, but he was still a wild animal and wary. She was well aware that he had the potential to be extremely dangerous. Both wolves were hungry. She didn't want to end up being their meal instead of the chicken, so she always kept a gun on her just to be on the safe side.

Standing out back, Angela heaved one of the chicken halves as far as she could. Bardolph paused, looking around briefly to see if it was safe. Finally satisfied, he came closer and snatched up the chicken. He carried it back in his mouth and placed it before the female wolf as she emerged from the shadows. Bardolph quickly returned to retrieve the second half when Angela tossed it toward him.

Each holding a prize, the wolves quickly retreated into the edge of the forest. Angela was pretty sure Bardolph's mate was carrying pups and that was why he had sought out her place. When he had been recovering from being shot, Angela had fed him raw chicken. Now he had a mate and she needed food.

Although the woods surrounding Angela's place were vast, food was still hard to come by. A pregnant female wolf would need to eat. When they eventually took a deer, or caught small animals, Angela knew they would stop coming around. Wolves would rather fend for themselves than have any contact with people. Until then, Angela was a source of food they could count on when they needed it.

Watching them as they vanished into the woods, she marveled at the rare privilege of seeing such magnificent, wild creatures. Not many people would ever have the chance she did to experience such things. It was just one more reason her place was so important to her, and why she never let people come around. She wanted to keep her place wild and special.

Angela stood in the doorway for a time, gazing off into the dark woods. She couldn't see the wolves anymore, but she knew they were out there, somewhere. When she heard one of them let out a long, wild howl, she smiled and went back inside to finish cooking her own dinner.

Chapter 7

Angela looked up from mixing a couple of drinks and saw Wanda swoop in the door looking hurried. Angela sighed inwardly with relief that help had arrived. She had been wondering if it would. Barry had, too. He was on the edge again with Wanda.

For the last several weeks she had been showing up when she was scheduled. Angela suspected it was because Ricky Sparling had become a regular on Wanda's nights. When she missed the start of this shift, Angela had begun to worry that she had fallen off the "no drama" wagon. Thankfully she was only late.

"Good," Barry said as he passed behind Angela. "Crazy Wanda has graced us with her royal presence."

"She's only a little late," Angela said, wondering as she said it why she was defending her.

Wanda came around behind the bar and put her purse under the counter. "Sorry I'm late," she said, catching her breath. "I ran into Albert out in the parking lot."

Angela put the two mixed drinks on a tray. "Well, you're here just in time to take this to table twelve."

Angela watched Wanda saunter among the tables to the calls and whistles of a few men. She swung her hips in a show as she lifted an arm and twirled a hand in appreciation of her fans. Wanda had arrived, the party could begin. She set the drinks down and whispered in the ear of one of the men. He laughed and swatted her bottom as she left.

When she returned with the empty tray and a big grin, she handed it across the bar to Angela. "They said you might as well start making them a second round."

Angela smiled to herself at Wanda's sales ability.

Wanda leaned in to be heard over the music. "So, he said that you would give me the twenty back."

Angela collected an empty and quickly wiped down the bar as a man left. "What are you talking about?"

"Albert," Wanda said, as if that was explanation enough.

Angela frowned as she pulled a couple of bottles from the cooler for an order. "Who the hell is Albert?"

Wanda leaned farther in on the bar. "Don't be silly."

"I'm not being silly. I don't know an Albert."

"Albert," Wanda repeated as if Angela was being dense. "You know, Albert. Your father."

Angela straightened. "What?"

"Your father. Albert." She flicked her hand over her shoulder toward the door. "I saw him in the parking lot."

"Old guy, leather ball cap? Riding a pink girl's bike?"

"That's him. Looks like he's down on his luck. He asked for a twenty. Real nice like. He said that he didn't want to come in and bother you while you were working and that you would pay me back."

Angela was instantly fuming. "You gave him money?"

Wanda looked puzzled. "He's your father, isn't he? He looked like he's run into hard times. He said he knew you were busy and asked if I could give him a twenty. He said, 'My daughter will gladly pay you back.'"

Angela could feel her face heat with anger. "You gave that junkie money?"

"Well, yeah. Like I said, he told me he was your dad."

Angela threw the towel down beside the sink. "I'll be right back."

Angela hurried through the crowded bar and raced out into the parking lot. She stopped and looked around. She spotted him leaning against her truck, smoking a cigarette. His bike was lying on the ground.

As Angela marched toward him, he saw her coming and quickly picked up his bicycle. He put the cigarette between his lips and hopped on his bike. Angela raced across the lot, but he was already pedaling away. He glanced back over his shoulder once, lifted his arm high to give her the finger, and then was gone down the road, happy that she knew he'd gotten back at her.

Back inside, Wanda returned to the bar after delivering drinks. "What was that all about?"

"That bum isn't my father." Angela pulled four five-dollar bills out of her tip pocket. "Here. He conned you out of this. It's not your fault. You were just being nice."

Wanda looked a bit confused. "He said he was your father."

"I know, but he was only saying that to get money so he could get himself some booze or maybe some arm candy."

Wanda shrugged as she stuffed the cash into a pocket. She looked a bit confused. "Are you sure?"

Angela let out a deep breath. "My mother's a drug addict. Whoever got her pregnant with me could be any one of the other addicts she slept with. There were plenty of possibilities. I suppose it's not out of the question that he could have been the one who got her pregnant."

"Oh. Well, sorry."

"Not your fault, but don't give him money anymore unless you don't expect me to pay you back. I work too hard to throw my money away on panhandlers."

Wanda turned when she saw Ricky Sparling coming in the door. "There's my guy." She was suddenly all sparkles and grins. "I have to go say hi."

Angela caught her arm. "Your guy? Wanda, have you forgotten? Ricky Sparling is married."

"I know. But he's taking care of that."

Angela let the woman's arm go. "You're just asking for grief." Even as she said it, she knew it was wasted effort.

"Don't worry. We'll be able to be together soon."

With that she hurried off to sit on Ricky's lap as she gave him a big kiss that earned a scattering of applause. Ricky had taken a table in the corner where he could watch Wanda go about her job. Angela thought he looked like a lost puppy waiting patiently for affection. Little did he know exactly what kind of woman had a leash around his neck.

Later that night, when the crowd had thinned, Wanda came up to the bar and leaned over close. "I'm going to take a short break. Cover for me, okay?"

Before Angela could agree, Wanda had already danced over to Ricky and grabbed his hand. She pulled him outside with her.

Angela forgot all about it until twenty or thirty minutes later when Wanda floated back in. All smiles, she leaned over the bar toward Angela to be heard over the music.

"I'm back," she said, still catching her breath. "I had to take care of my man." She winked at Angela as she reached for a tray of drinks that needed to be delivered.

Angela put a hand on her arm to stop her. "You better go fix your lipstick, first. It's all over your face."

Wanda giggled as if embarrassed, which she was not. "Oops. Thanks." She left the tray and hurried toward the bathroom.

CHAPTER 8

Wanda breathlessly pulled Ricky's hand out from under her tank top.

"What's wrong?" he asked, equally breathlessly.

"I have to get home to bed." That was a lie, of course, but she was growing irritated with the stalled progress of their relationship. She had thought that by now he would have rid himself of his wife and they would be able to move in together in his nice house in a nice part of town. She'd driven past it a number of times, dreaming.

He smiled and started kissing her neck while pushing his hand under her top again. "That sounds good to me."

She pushed him off her. "It sounds good to me, too. It sounds a lot better than the backseat of your Suburban. But I've already told you a dozen times that you can't come to my parents' house. They're crazy religious. They would never allow a man to be there with me. They would think you were the devil. My father would go berserk and probably beat the both of us."

"Well, we could go up to the Riley Motel."

"With the prostitutes turning tricks? You really want people to think I'm a whore?"

"No, of course not—"

"Maybe that's all I really am to you. A whore you can bang."

"Babe, no, don't say that. You know I love you. It's just that you said you were going to get a place of your own. When you do we could go there, and we wouldn't have to go to a motel where people would think less of you."

Wanda fussed with her hair, trying to get it back into place. The parking lot outside the bar was empty except for her car and Ricky's big Suburban, which he had parked out back.

"And you said that you were going to be filing papers to divorce her. You've been saying it for a month, now, that once you filed the papers she would be out and then I could move in with you. Why should I get a place if I'm going to be moving in with you?"

Ricky sat back. "Babe, you know I'm trying to handle it. My wife is giving me all kinds of grief. She's a witch on wheels. I hate her. I wish she would just drop dead."

Wanda stared at him, liking the thought. "So, you still haven't filed the papers?"

"Well, no, not exactly. You know how it is. First things first. I'll think of something. I promise."

"What about the private detective? Hasn't he gotten anything on her yet?"

Ricky hesitated. "He will, babe. I'm sure he will. In the meantime, I have to play it cool, you know? We have to be careful. If my wife caught us together she would be able to throw me out and she would get everything."

"What do you have that makes that much of a difference? You don't have kids. You have a job, she can get a job. You just split things up and each go your separate way. You pull down good money with your business. You can get another place. Then we'd be done with her and we could be together. That's what you're always telling me you want."

"And I do want that, but she'll take the house if I don't get something on her, first."

Wanda shrugged. "So what? You make good money. She'd be out of the picture and then we could get a new place and be together. That's what matters."

"But my parents left me the house. It's paid off. It's worth a lot. I don't want to lose it. Our marriage has been over for a long time and I've told her we should split up, but she won't go along with getting a divorce. She said that I should just go right ahead and leave her if that's what I want and then she'll get the house and a nice big alimony check every week. Damn, Wanda, she would get half of what my business is worth. You know how hard I've worked for what I have. She hasn't done a damn thing for the business. She just sits on her ass, but she'd still get half of it."

"And that's what matters to you? Is that more important than us being together?"

"Well, no, but..."

"If you really loved me you'd get her out of your life—one way or another. You're a big strong guy. You need to man up and stop letting her push you around."

"I know, babe, but let's talk about it later, okay?"

She pushed him away when he tried to get on top of her. "You're pussy whipped. I have to go home and get some sleep and think about where my life is going. I thought it was going to be with you, but now you're making me doubt that you're man enough to do what needs to be done. Maybe I need to find me a real man."

"Come on, babe, don't be like that. You know I love you and all I want is to be with you."

"If you really mean that, Ricky, then you would have the balls to do something about it. There are other ways to get rid of her besides divorce."

He wasn't getting the hint. She could see that sooner or later she was going to have to lay it all out for him. If she was going to have him and his big house in a nice part of town, she was going to have to take charge and tell him what to do. She knew how to make men do what she wanted.

"It won't be much longer, I promise. I'll call the detective in the morning and see if he has anything yet. I know she's cheating on me. I just need him to catch her at it and then I can file for divorce and have her kicked out. Then we will have the house with her out of the picture and she won't get anything."

Out of the picture was exactly what Wanda wanted.

"How much longer is that going to take?"

He ran a hand back over his face. "Not much longer. I promise."

Wanda knew that the whole detective thing was a dead end, but for the time being she had to play along. Once it fell through she would exert her control over him and then solve the problem once and for all.

Wanda opened the door. "It had better not, Ricky. I'm getting sick and tired of this. If you want to be with me, then you need to get rid of the bitch. The backseat of your truck isn't my idea of how I want to be together with the man I love. I thought you loved me, too. Or maybe you just want to get laid?"

"No, no, I swear. It's not like that. I do love you, I swear." He tried to put his arm around her, but she twisted out of his embrace and stepped down to the pavement. She leaned back in.

"If you really mean that, then one way or another, you need to get rid of her, understand?"

He nodded. "Okay, I'll think of something."

Wanda had already thought of something.

CHAPTER 9

Wanda was in a dead sleep when someone pounding on the front door brought her half awake. She could tell by the light leaking in around the curtain that it was midmorning. When she came home from working late at the bar, she usually slept at least until noon. She knew it couldn't be noon, yet. She groaned and rolled over, hoping the racket would end so she could drop back into the balm of sleep.

Then she heard a woman yelling. Wanda didn't recognize the voice. Probably someone from their church, or maybe a neighbor. She heard her father saying something to try to calm the woman down, but he started getting angry himself.

Despite all his talk of God and the true path and seeking the Lord's guidance, her father had a mean streak. His angry fits could last for hours. Afterward, he sometimes felt guilty and spent hours praying with Wanda's mother, trying to smooth over the scene he'd made, asking the Lord for forgiveness.

There had been plenty of times when Wanda had been little when he'd flown into a rage and beaten her. She couldn't remember having deserved it, but she could clearly remember the injustice of times when he accused her of things she hadn't done and then whipped her with his belt.

A number of times he accused her of serving the devil and tried to beat the evil out of her. Her mother never lifted a finger to stop the beatings. When she had been in tears afterward, her mother not only never tried to soothe her, but treated her with cold indifference.

God might have forgiven the both of them, but Wanda never had.

She knew that her father wouldn't dare lay a finger on her now. The last time he'd flown into a rage over some boy she had been seeing and yanked his belt free of his pants, she had leaned in and said, "Go ahead and do it. Then I'll call the police. I'm underage. You'll go to jail. Social service will take me out of this hellhole. What will people in your church think of you then?" That had wilted his fit.

When there was an urgent knock at her bedroom door, Wanda sat up and rubbed her eyes. "What!"

Her mother pushed open the door. Wanda could see her dark shape in the dim light of the hallway.

"Wanda, you had better get out here. There's a woman out here demanding to see you."

Wanda flopped back on the bed. "Whoever it is, tell her to go away."

Her mother came to the bed and shook her arm. "Wanda, get out there, now!"

Wanda could tell by her mother's tone that she wasn't going to let it go, so Wanda swung her legs around and put her feet on the floor. She sat on the edge of the bed as she stretched and yawned. Her mother threw her robe at her.

"Here. Put this on. Hurry up."

She didn't know what her mother could be so upset about, but Wanda was getting angry. She didn't like being woken up, especially by her parents. She was an adult. She didn't want her parents coming into her room anymore. By the time she had her robe on, she was in a murderous mood.

She threw the robe closed and tied it as she hurried down the dark hall. All the curtains in the house were still drawn, so it had to be early morning. The front door stood open. Wanda saw a rather chunky woman in ugly jeans that showed off a bulging belly and a broad, fat ass. Her short, curly hair made her look twice what was probably her true age. She stood with her fists on her hips as she glared, watching Wanda come into the room.

Wanda's father held an arm out. "This young woman would like to speak with you."

Wanda frowned. "Who are you, and what the hell do you want this early in the morning?"

The woman charged right up into Wanda's face. "I'm Ricky Sparling's wife, that's who the hell I am!"

Wanda shoved her back. "So what?"

"I heard you're the whore he's been screwing."

"Who told you that?"

"It doesn't matter who told me. I know it's true!"

"And how would you know it's true?" Wanda scoffed.

"Because when I asked Ricky if it was true he was screwing a cheap tramp named Wanda from the bar he goes to, he got that shit-eating expression on his face and he couldn't look me in the eye. He couldn't even come up with a lie. He knew he'd been caught, and I knew that what I'd been told was true."

Before Wanda could say anything, the woman shook her finger right in Wanda's face. "If you come sniffing around him again I'm going to strangle the life out of you! Got it, bitch?"

The woman didn't wait for an answer. She stormed out the open door and down the walk to her car. The tires squealed as she sped away.

Wanda's father quietly closed the front door.

With a grim look, her mother folded her arms. "Well?"

Wanda glared. "Well, what?"

"Is that woman's husband cheating on her with you?"

"Why don't you two mind your own business?"

"You're living in our house, so it is our business!" her father yelled. "Adultery is a serious sin! It's a sign that the devil works through you!"

"Fuck off," Wanda said as she turned toward her room.

"Wanda!" her mother called after her. "We won't have you speak to us in that way. You will show us proper respect."

Wanda rolled her eyes as she started toward her room. Her father grabbed her by the arm hard enough to leave bruises. He yanked her back around. "You heard me. As long as you live under our roof, you are going to live a God-fearing life."

"I told you, I'm going to get my own place, so you don't need to worry about it."

"When? It had better be soon. We aren't going to put up with you bringing evil into our home."

"I'm leaving as soon as I get dressed. Is that soon enough for you? I don't need any more crap from the two of you."

"As soon as you leave, I'm going to have the locks changed. When you accept the Lord as your savior and renounce your sinful ways then we'll allow you to come home again, but not before!"

Wanda was too angry to say anything, so she marched off and slammed the door to her room.

As she pulled out a suitcase she tried to think who could have told Ricky's wife about them. Ricky had always said that they needed to be careful until he could get something on her so he could be the one to file for divorce. Who knew about them?

Wanda paused from stuffing clothes in the suitcase and straightened. She suddenly realized who it had to be. There was only one person who could have told Ricky's wife that he was seeing Wanda. It couldn't be. But it had to be true.

Wanda's anger turned white hot.

CHAPTER 10

Wanda left her parents' house as soon as she had packed a couple of suitcases and stuffed some shoes, hair products, and her makeup case into tote bags. Her parents were still in the living room, still ranting about Wanda's sins. She ignored them on her way out. She could hear the front door being locked behind her.

She drove around for a while, seething over the betrayal, furious over what Ricky's wife had said to her. The nerve of the woman had Wanda gritting her teeth in a rage and squeezing the life out of the steering wheel.

She had no place to stay and no one to stay with, so she got a room at the Riley Motel. The place was a dump, but it was by-the-week and cheap, which was all she could afford, and besides, she didn't plan on living there long. She was sick and tired of waiting on other people to make the changes that needed to be made. It was time for her to take control and set things right.

Ricky wasn't ever going to do what needed doing on his own. He didn't have the necessary initiative. Fortunately, Ricky was pliable as putty. She simply needed to mold him to do what needed to be done.

It wasn't her night to work. It was Angela's night, though. Wanda was livid that someone had gone behind her back and told Ricky's wife about them. It complicated things.

There was only one person it could be: Angela.

Angela was always reminding her that Ricky was married. Wanda had thought she and Angela were friends. It was hard to believe that Angela would stab her in the back like this. It had to be that she was jealous of what Wanda had with Ricky. Otherwise a friend wouldn't go behind a friend's back and double-cross them.

The more she thought about the betrayal the angrier she became. She couldn't get it out of her mind. The way Ricky's wife had barged in on Wanda was humiliating. All because Angela had betrayed her.

Once it was dark, she drove down the long hill and cruised through the parking lot of Barry's Place. She saw Angela's pickup parked there, but not finding who she was looking for she kept going, trying to think of where he could be. She drove slowly through the parking lot of a small nearby strip mall, but didn't see him there, either. Since he seemed to hang around the bar a lot, she went back there, thinking he might have shown up by then. No luck. She drove slowly through a couple of neighborhoods known for drugs, but he was nowhere to be seen.

On her way back to the bar again she finally spotted him at a liquor store. He was leaning up against the wall on the darker side of the building, smoking a cigarette and drinking from a bottle in a brown paper bag. His pink bicycle was leaned up against the wall next to him. He was alone.

Wanda parked right in front of him and shut off the engine. He watched warily as she got out of her car, ready to bolt if it turned out to be trouble.

"Albert?"

He looked even more ready to run.

"Albert, I'm a friend of Angela's. Your daughter. Remember? I gave you a twenty one night in the parking lot of Barry's Place."

He finally nodded that he remembered. "What do you want? I can't give you the twenty back. I told you to get it from my daughter."

Wanda smiled as she approached. "I know. Angela already paid me back for the money I gave you."

"Good," he said, still wary. "I told you she would."

"I was wondering if you'd like to earn some more money."

He used a thumb to push the bill of his leather ball cap up a little as he frowned at her. "What did you have in mind?"

"I just need some information. I'm willing to pay you for it."

"How much?"

Wanda shrugged. "Depends on how helpful you can be."

He stood up away from the building and looked around suspiciously, fearing it might be some kind of trap.

"What could I possibly tell you that you'd pay me for?"

"You said that Angela is your daughter. She says otherwise."

"So?"

"So, if you really are her father, it seems to me like you would know where she lives."

He took off the cap and scratched his scalp as he thought. What sparse hair he had was gray and wispy thin. He looked up.

"I used to hang around with Sally, Angela's mother. When Angela was young she often went to stay with her grandparents at their place out in the countryside. It was way out in the mountains. Could that be the place you mean?"

Wanda smiled. Angela had told her that her grandfather had built the house she lived in. "That's the place. Do you know where it is?"

He squinted out into the darkness. He looked back at her.

"How much is this information worth to you?"

"How much do you want for it?"

"A hundred bucks."

Wanda considered a moment. "All right. Tell me where it is and I'll give you a hundred dollars."

He scratched his cheek. "I grew up in Milford Falls, so I tend to know where everything is. I have the general idea of the area in my head, but I can't remember well enough that I could give you exact directions. I'd have to drive around with you until I recognized the correct roads."

"Okay. Put your bike in the back of my car and let's go."

He leaned back against the building and folded his arms. "You just asked if I knew. A guided tour of the back roads to find her place will cost you an extra twenty."

Wanda leaned back in the car for her billfold and took out three twenties. Just by his facial features, she didn't really believe that he was Angela's father, but if he knew where Angela lived, that was good enough. She held the twenties out to him.

"Half now and the other half once you show me her place."

He studied the money in her hand, then her eyes, and then he took the cash. He folded it and stuffed it into a pocket.

"When do you want to go there?"

Angela was at work, so Wanda knew she wouldn't be home for hours and hours. "I want to go now."

He nodded once. "All right, then. You open the hatch of your car and I'll put my bike in."

CHAPTER 11

After a long shift at the bar, Angela was looking forward to some solitude and some sleep. Brandy, the girl who alternated with Wanda on her nights off, was a lot less tiring to work with. She was cheerful, friendly, and efficient. More importantly, she was not subject to the same dark moods that could make for a long night.

But then Barry had told her that Wanda had called in and quit. It was Wanda's regular night off, as was the next night, so at least it gave Barry a couple of days to hire a replacement. He said that a woman, Tiffany, had come in asking about work, and that she seemed like a good fit for the spot. Angela was glad she wasn't going to have to handle things alone, although she had done that enough not to be worried about it. She was puzzled, though, as to why Wanda would simply up and quit.

After she parked her pickup in front of her house and shut off the engine, Angela put her head back against the headrest for a moment, just to enjoy the silence. When Bardolph howled, she smiled. She was excited that she would be able to get a glimpse of him and his mate. Seeing such magnificent creatures was always a treat.

Once inside, she took out a couple of half chickens and set them on the counter while changing out of her work clothes. She was looking forward to a hot shower and a good night's sleep, but first she wanted to take the chicken out to the wolves.

Angela took one of the chicken halves out the back door in her left hand. In her other hand she carried a gun, as she always did.

Even though they accepted a handout of raw chicken, they were still wild animals and Angela knew better than to assume they weren't dangerous. Angela wasn't so much worried about Bardolph, because he knew her, but the female had shown herself to be aggressive. Being pregnant probably only made her more edgy.

As Angela walked out into the moonlit backyard, she spotted Bardolph sitting back at the edge of the woods. He let out a long, mournful howl. Angela frowned at how different it sounded from his usual howls.

And then she suddenly saw why.

Angela had almost stepped on the female wolf lying dead at her feet.

In sudden shock and dismay, Angela knelt down beside the dead animal. It had an entry wound through the front of its chest, exiting out the back where the damage was extensive. It seemed clear that someone had shot the wolf with a large-caliber weapon.

Angela ran her hand over the lifeless pups in the dead female's cold womb. "I'm so sorry," she whispered.

She'd been delighted that Bardolph had found a mate so that he wouldn't be alone, and that they were going to have pups. But now someone had unexpectedly put an end to it.

It was shocking that the wolf had been shot and killed, but what was even more alarming was that someone with a gun had been on her property and close up by her house.

Angela stood with her own gun in hand and looked around, searching the shadows, feeling unexpectedly vulnerable. She didn't see anyone, but that didn't mean they couldn't still be there. She felt violated that someone had invaded her private sanctuary.

She went back inside and retrieved a flashlight. She inspected the backyard but didn't see any signs of who had been there. Since there was grass, rock, moss, and small brush, she wouldn't necessarily expect there to be footprints, so she wasn't all that surprised when she found none.

She next walked down the drive, searching from side to side for tracks of any kind. Here and there, in the gravel, was a random footprint or two where the intruder had stepped off the grass onto the side of the road in order to avoid brush. The gravel was too dry and loose for clear footprints, but she could tell by the different sizes of the prints that they were from two different people.

Out at the road, on the other side of her barbed-wire fence and the cable across the drive, she found tire marks where a vehicle had pulled off the road and parked. It looked to be a relatively small car. Stretching up and looking in both directions, Angela didn't see any sign of it.

When she spotted something in the beam of her flashlight, she squatted down and found the stub of an unfiltered cigarette. It was just beside the tire tracks where the car had pulled off the road and stopped. The cigarette was on the passenger side. There was a footprint that made it clear the passenger had gotten out and snubbed out the cigarette with a shoe.

With nothing to be found other than the crushed cigarette and no one around, Angela finally made her way back up the road to the house. The tracks seemed to indicate they had deliberately pulled off the road and parked at the bottom of her drive. When they had walked up the drive and gone around the back of the house, the wolf had probably come out of the woods, possibly viewing the person as prey or a threat, and had been shot.

It was puzzling that the house hadn't been touched. She wondered if they had been spooked by the wolf and left, fearing that someone might have heard the gunshot.

With a heavy heart, Angela retrieved a shovel and went about digging a hole near the woods. It was hard going through roots. She had to pry out rocks and toss them aside, but she was animated by her anger over the wolf having been killed, as well as the vulnerable feeling of someone having been right there around her house. At least they hadn't broken in.

When the hole was deep enough, she grabbed the two hind legs and dragged the dead animal into the hole. With the back of her hand, she wiped tears from her cheek, and then she started shoveling the dirt into the grave.

Bardolph watched from the shadows among the trees. He howled once. When she had finished shoveling in all the dirt, she knelt down and used her hands to pat the dirt down.

As she did, Bardolph came close and slowly walked past her, brushing his side against her before sniffing the grave. He seemed to understand that his mate was gone.

He moved to the other side of the grave, lay down, and rested his head on top of the fresh dirt, as if he intended to hold vigil. Together they grieved for the dead wolf, and all that could have been.

Chapter 12

Wanda had been waiting in the parking lot not far from Ricky's house for an hour. She was annoyed that he still hadn't called. She had spent the last two weeks on the phone, reminding him how terrible it would be for him if his wife divorced him and how it was only a matter of time, now that she'd been told he was cheating. He would lose his house. He would have to pay a good chunk of his income to her for alimony. It could jeopardize his business. She would be a leech, sucking him dry, for the rest of his life.

Wanda had hammered home how a divorce would ruin his life, and how in turn it would ruin their lives together. To keep that from happening, they simply needed to get rid of her.

Wanda had kept Ricky at arm's length while stoking the furnace of his fears. Wanda had wanted him aching for her until he finally saw that her way was the only way.

But he was an hour late in calling her. If he chickened out on her now she was going to be a lot more than simply angry with him. She had invested too much time in this for him to have second thoughts.

At last the phone rang. It was Ricky.

"Well?"

"She's finally asleep," he said, sounding frazzled. "It took a lot longer than we thought it would. She wanted to stay up and watch TV. So I made her another drink. I dissolved a couple more Valium in it. It took a while, but she's finally out."

"Good. I'll be there in five minutes."

Wanda was excited to get it over and done with. She had to force herself to drive the speed limit through the nice part of town. The last thing she needed was to get pulled over by the police.

She yearned to live in such a nice area. Her parents' house was a dump in a dumpy part of town. Her father had a low-paying job cleaning vehicles at a trucking company. If that wasn't bad enough, he gave a portion of his income to the church. He always said that it was God's house that mattered, not theirs.

After a lifetime of putting up with her parents' fanaticism and living in a run-down, dangerous part of town, and now living by the week in the wretched Riley Motel, Wanda deserved better. Now, it was finally within reach.

As she came around the corner, past some beautiful maple trees, she saw that the garage door was open. She'd driven past his house a number of times before. It was the kind of house she'd dreamed of since she was a girl. A real pretty house with shutters. A real pretty house with a nice yard. A real pretty house with a good-looking husband to take care of her.

Ricky was walking back and forth inside the garage, waiting, looking nervous as hell. She smiled as she parked off to the side, out of the way so he would be able to get his big Suburban out of the garage. Given how he was pacing, she thought that maybe she should have told him to take one of the Valium himself.

"Do you have it?" she asked as she met him in the garage.

He held up a big, heavy-duty, milky-white nylon cable tie as he pushed the button to lower the garage door. "What if she wakes up?"

"There's two of us and one of her. What's she gonna do? She's too drugged to be able to put up much of a fight." Wanda smiled. "She'll probably sleep through the whole thing."

Ricky paced anxiously. "Maybe we should just have used the pills. You know, given her enough of an overdose to stop her breathing. Made it look like suicide."

"Did you have an easy time getting half a dozen Valium into her?"

"Hell no. Why do you think it took so long?"

"Then how would you have gotten her to swallow half a bottle of them?"

He made a face. "Yeah, I guess you're right."

"You know I'm right. We've talked about this, Ricky."

She swept an arm around his neck and pulled him down to give him a passionate kiss. That did the trick. He put his arms around her and pulled her close to return the kiss.

"It's been too long," he said, his voice thick with desire.

"Well, when we get done with this business we can go to bed. Together. In our house."

"At last," he said, smiling. "I can't tell you how much of a relief it was to have her asleep after our big fight."

"What big fight?"

"She was yelling and screaming, still pissed over finding out about us. She said she was going to divorce my ass and have everything. I told her that she was wrong, that there was nothing serious going on, and whoever told her I was cheating on her didn't know what they were talking about."

Wanda wasn't listening very intently. As she looked around the garage she was smiling over what was to come. Her parents' house wasn't big enough to have a garage, much less a garage with room for cabinets and a workbench.

"I presume she didn't believe you."

"Hell no," he said. "It made her even more angry that I was denying it. She said then that she knew it was true because the old guy told her that he had seen us butt-naked in the back of my Suburban parked behind the bar."

Wanda frowned as she turned back. "What are you talking about? What old guy?"

Ricky threw up his hands in exasperation. "She said she was suspicious of why I spent so much time at that bar, so she went there to see if she could catch me with someone, but before she went in she met this old guy in the parking lot, a guy on a pink bicycle. She asked him if he knew the man who had the big muddy Suburban. He said that for fifty dollars he'd tell what he knew. She gave him the cash and he told her, then, that he'd seen me together a lot with a woman named Wanda who works there in the bar. He told her that after the bar closed one night he saw us going at it in the back of my truck."

Wanda stood staring in shock.

"She said she went into the bar the next morning when I was at work and told the owner she was a friend of Wanda's and wanted to know where she lived so she could drop off some things she had borrowed. I guess Barry told her where you were living with your parents at the time."

That conniving bitch had made Wanda believe it was Angela who had told her, and all along it had been that bum, Albert. Wanda had gone to Angela's house to get even for the betrayal, intent on spray-painting some names on her door, and then maybe shooting the place up. It had been dark out in the countryside and they could hardly see.

Before she could do what she had intended, Angela's dog suddenly appeared out of the darkness, snarling viciously at her. She instinctively pointed the gun and pulled the trigger. She hadn't expected the force of the kickback from Brad's .357. It nearly knocked her on her ass. The sound had nearly deafened her.

After recovering from the shock of the recoil and noise, she had seen in the moonlight that Angela's dog was dead. She had figured that was even better revenge than she had intended, so they had left.

"I made a drink for her with a couple pills in it," Ricky was saying, "and told her that I was sorry and that I'd make it up to her. I apologized and begged like crazy for her forgiveness. I put on quite an act convincing her I was sincere and to have a drink with me, then another. She finally calmed down. After the drinks she was slipping into a mellow mood and wanted to watch TV before going to bed. She could hardly keep her eyes open as it was, but she didn't want to go to bed. I didn't know what to do and I was afraid of making her angry, so I made her another drink and put a couple more pills in it."

Wanda was hardly listening. She was outraged that it had been Albert all along who had blabbed everything to Ricky's wife. Wanda wanted to strangle the little snitch for making her believe it was Angela who had betrayed her, when all along it had been him. He hadn't said a word about any of it as he directed her to Angela's house out in the desolate mountains.

"Let's get on with it," Wanda said, to stop Ricky from rambling on with the story. It was clear his wife had rattled him. Wanda knew he was on the verge of chickening out, so she turned him around and give him a little shove toward the door into the house.

As Ricky led her through the dimly lit house, Wanda looked around with wide eyes. She'd never been in a house that nice. The carpet was plush underfoot. The furniture looked expensive. There was a huge TV on the wall. Ricky walked on tiptoes ahead of her, as if he might wake his wife and she would come out of the bedroom with a baseball bat.

When they reached the end of the hallway, he quietly pushed open the door and stood aside to let Wanda see his wife sprawled on her back on the bed, her arms splayed out, one leg hanging off the side of the mattress. She was fully clothed in those same kind of jeans that displayed her big belly and fat ass. Wanda had a hard time understanding how a good-looking guy like Ricky ever ended up with such a pig.

"Hurry up," Wanda urged.

Ricky looked back at her, then went in and put one knee on the bed to lean over his wife. He pulled the heavy-duty cable tie from his pocket and slipped it around her neck like a necklace. She moaned but didn't open her eyes.

Wanda stood beside the bed and watched him feed the end of the cable tie through the ratchet mechanism. He grunted as he pulled it tight.

When he did, his wife started to have difficulty breathing. She opened her eyes as she urgently tried to suck in air. It made an awful sound as she struggled to breathe in and out through the constriction.

"Pull it tighter," Wanda told him, "it's not tight enough."

He grunted with the effort. "I'm pulling it as tight as I can. My fingers keep sliding off. I can't get a good grip."

"I'll be right back," Wanda said.

"She's trying to get up!"

Wanda rolled her eyes at having to explain everything to him. "Put your knee on her damn chest."

While he followed her instructions, Wanda raced out of the bedroom, down the hall, and back to the garage. She snatched up a pair of pliers she had seen before on the workbench and ran back to the bedroom.

When she got there, Ricky was trying to hold his wife down on the bed with a knee. She was clawing at him as she made a horrible sucking sound trying to breathe.

"Here," Wanda told him, "use these to pull it tight."

Ricky grabbed the tail of the cable tie with the pliers and, while pressing the heel of his hand against the catch at the side of her throat, pulled more through. It made a ratcheting sound as he pulled it tighter, locking it down ever harder. It bunched up her skin as it dug deep into her fleshy neck. His wife reached up, trying to get one hand around his throat as she clawed at the nylon cable tie around her neck with the other.

"Tighter!" Wanda yelled.

He gritted his teeth with the effort of yanking it tighter. It clicked a few times with each hard pull.

No longer able to get any air, the woman opened her eyes wide in terror that overcame the booze and drugs. She was now wide awake and in mortal fear.

Wanda leaned in over her. "Remember when you said you were going to strangle the life out of me, bitch? Well, I guess you're the one having the life strangled out of her."

As she stared wide-eyed at Wanda, Wanda spit in her face.

Her arms flailed weakly. As her face began to turn blue, her arms slowed down, and after a last swipe at her husband, they flopped down on the bed.

Standing close together, Ricky and Wanda watched as his wife's body convulsed a few times before it finally went still. Her lips were a blackish blue. Her bulging eyes remained open, but they no longer saw anything.

Wanda felt a giddy wave of satisfaction at getting back at the woman for the scene she'd made in front of Wanda's parents. Wanda smiled wider when she saw that the woman had pissed her pants.

It had been such an exhilarating experience that she was a bit sad it was over.

Together they checked her pockets to make sure she didn't have any identification on her; then they rolled the dead woman up in a blanket and tied rope around it. It wasn't easy, but they managed to lug her dead weight out to the garage. Ricky opened the back of the truck and they hoisted her in.

"See? Easy," Wanda said. "No blood, no evidence."

They went back to the bedroom and stuffed a bunch of the dead woman's clothes and shoes into black plastic garbage bags. Before putting the purse in one of the bags, they took out the keys and all the identification along with a few receipts. They would burn the bags of clothes, but to be on the safe side they wanted to destroy the identification separately in order to be certain that nothing was left. Wanda put the house key in her own pocket.

Ricky's wife didn't have any relatives in Milford Falls. All of her family lived in California. There would be no one to report her missing. If anyone ever called to inquire about her, Ricky's story would be that their marriage had been falling apart for some time and after a big argument, she'd packed most of her things and left him. He would say that he didn't know where she had gone but assumed back to California.

Once they had loaded everything into the Suburban, they were finally on their way. As they drove through town, Wanda took the SIM card out of the dead woman's phone, folded it back and forth until it broke apart, then tossed the pieces out the window one at a time. She twisted the phone until it broke and threw it in the river as they crossed a bridge.

Ricky worked in the forests that surrounded Milford Falls, so he knew all the back roads and remote areas. It was late, so there was little traffic. Once they made their way out of town they didn't see any cars. They drove for nearly an hour down increasingly narrow roads, ending up on a dirt road across private property where he had recently cut trees.

He finally stopped in a place with a steep drop-off down into a ravine. The road on the large private property had only been used by his logging crew, so no one would come this far out.

They pulled the dead woman out of the truck and pushed her over the edge. Ricky watched with a flashlight to make sure she went far down the rocky hillside into an inaccessible spot. Leaves and forest debris that the body disturbed tumbled down to cover the corpse.

Once they had disposed of the body, they drove back to the yard of Ricky's business. It was located in a remote area just out of town so it would be closer to the woods where they worked. The parked log trucks and other equipment made the place look ghostly in the moonlight.

Ricky poured some gasoline in two of the big burn barrels where they sometimes burned brush, then pulled clothes out of the bags and tossed them in one at a time so they would burn better. He occasionally tossed in some branches to help keep a fire going so it would burn everything completely. They stood together, his arm around her, as they watched the fires burn. Every once in a while, he would add more clothes and fuel to make sure everything was reduced to ashes.

Wanda couldn't wait to get home to her new house.

CHAPTER 13

The first night in her new home was exciting. The sex was fantastic, although Ricky seemed distracted. Once she made sure he was well satisfied and had fallen asleep, she explored her new home, marveling at the size of the rooms, the color-coordinated decorating, the quality of the fabrics on couch and chairs, and the beautiful chandelier on a dimmer switch in the dining room. She inspected the knickknacks and looked in closets. She ate leftover chicken she found in the refrigerator as she inspected the dishes in the cabinets and the silverware in the drawers.

Things were finally working out.

A couple of days later, Ricky sold his wife's car to some sleazy characters Wanda knew who dealt in stolen automobiles. Since it was a nearly new, common model, they were eager to have it. The price was dirt cheap on the condition that it never be found. They said they parted out the cars they hooked, so there was no worry of that. Wanda used some of the money to buy herself some new shoes she'd had her eye on.

It took some time, talking to people she knew who frequented bars, but Wanda finally found out where Albert lived. She was deeply angry that he had told Ricky's wife about them, leading to the scene at Wanda's parents' house, but worse, he had caused Wanda to believe that it had been Angela who had snitched. All that time she had spent with Albert, driving around on godforsaken roads through the woods until they found Angela's place, he had never once mentioned that he'd told Ricky's wife about her.

Because he'd kept that from her, she had mistakenly blamed Angela for betraying her, and as a result she had shot Angela's dog when it surprised her. She was angry at Albert about that. It turned out that Angela had had nothing to do with telling Ricky's wife about Wanda. It had been Albert's doing all along. Angela had been the one person Wanda had trusted, the one person she really cared about, and Wanda had shot her dog.

It had all been Albert's fault.

She had quit her job specifically because she had been so hurt, believing Angela had betrayed her, that she didn't want to see her ever again. It turned out she had nothing to do with it.

It had all been Albert's fault.

Now that Wanda was with Ricky, she didn't really need her job back, but she found that she really missed Angela in her life. She'd never missed anyone before. But she missed seeing Angela, missed talking to her.

Wanda wanted to get back in Angela's good graces. Angela represented some indescribable core in Wanda's life. Angela somehow made her want to do better. Angela had always been straight with her, always been honest. Angela always explained how she could get out of problems without calling her names or lecturing her the way her parents did. She just seemed to know the right thing to do when Wanda was completely bewildered as to how to get out of a jam. Angela had been a true friend when no one else cared enough to help her. And Wanda had shot her dog.

It had all been Albert's fault.

While she could never in a million years tell Angela what she had done, she did want to be friends with her again. She thought that maybe she could get her job back working at the bar with Angela and that would help mend their relationship.

The problem was, there was always a risk of that bastard Albert ratting on her and telling Angela that Wanda had been the one who had shot her dog. Albert had already betrayed her to Ricky's wife, so he obviously couldn't be trusted.

There was only one way to make sure he didn't talk.

She was going to have to kill him.

She had found out he was homeless—no surprise—and lived in a seedy part of town not far from Barry's Place, off in the woods in a ravine behind some small businesses along a busy street. There were a number of homeless encampments scattered through the area.

It was late in the day when she finally found Albert's lair. Tucked under scraggly trees and in among a tangle of brush was a tent of sorts made out of old blue plastic tarps. The roof was held up by ropes and twine strung to trees. The ground all around was littered with empty plastic bottles, food containers, and wine bottles, many of them broken. She suspected that the broken bottles were a poor man's barbed-wire fence. By the unmistakable, gagging smell, she knew he used the nearby bushes as his toilet.

Wanda leaned down and spotted his feet just inside the opening. He was asleep. Since he prowled at night, that made sense. She navigated her way through the burglar alarm of empty cans and bottles, through the minefield of broken glass, and stepped over his pink bicycle. Quiet as a mouse, she ducked down and went inside.

He was snoring in a deep sleep. Seeing used needles and empty booze bottles lying all over the dirt floor of his "home," she knew why he was sleeping so soundly. She relaxed, realizing that in a drugged state he wasn't liable to wake easily or be too alert once he did. She had to smile at how easy it was to deal with troublesome people when they were drunk or drugged.

Wanda had her big .357 Magnum revolver with her, but she was reluctant to use it unless absolutely necessary. She could always shoot him and then make a quick exit. Being a revolver, it had the advantage of not leaving shell casings, the way a semiauto would. Anyone seeing a well-dressed woman walking casually down the street wouldn't think the shot had come from her. She would simply act as surprised and confused as everyone else as she departed the area.

She saw a stained pillow off to the side and considered using that to muffle the gunshot. Not ideal, but better than nothing. That was, until she saw something better.

Albert was lying on his side. Just inside the back waistband of his filthy pants she spotted the handle of a knife sticking up.

When she yanked the knife out of the sheath, he snorted partially awake and flopped over on his back. Wanda immediately threw her leg over and straddled him to hold him down.

He opened his bloodshot eyes and blinked up at her in confusion.

"You little bastard," she growled down at him.

He looked left and right, then back up at her face looming over him. "What…Wanda?"

"That's right. The Wanda you lied to, the Wanda you tricked, the Wanda you double-crossed."

"What are you talking about?"

He sounded like he was getting angry. Good.

"You told Ricky's wife about us."

He frowned. "So what?"

"You led me to Angela's house and didn't say a thing when I told you how angry I was at her for betraying me. You never said a word about it being you all along. Because of you I shot her dog."

"Fuck you!"

Wanda, already on a hot boil, went over the edge. She slammed the knife into the side of his neck.

He grabbed her wrist as she yanked it back out, but the damage was done. He was not only old, but still in a fog from whatever he'd drunk or shot up.

Blood pumped out of the side of his neck in thick spurts. She moved her right leg back so it wouldn't get on her. His eyes wide, he gasped.

Wanda wrenched her wrist away from his weak grip and with both hands on the handle put the point of the blade at the base of his throat in the hollow of his neck. Looking into his eyes, she pounced over the knife with all of her weight, shoving the blade all the way in.

As she got up, she watched the pool of blood under his head grow larger and larger.

She smiled as his eyes grew big and round, looking at her in confusion the whole time he gasped, trying to get air, one hand over the spurting wound in the side of his neck, trying in vain to stop the bleeding, his other hand waving wildly, trying to snatch at her. Each long pull for air made a gurgling sound as it bubbled through the blood.

The question in his panicked eyes was obvious.

"Why?" she asked for him. "Because you made me betray my only friend. You made me betray Angela, the only person in my life who ever treated me decent. The only one. That's why."

He couldn't answer with the knife blade jammed down through his windpipe. He was too weak to pull the knife out and he couldn't stop the blood pumping out of him into the dirt floor of his pathetic hovel.

"You wasted your life, old man. If you really are Angela's father, you missed out on a lifetime of knowing her. You missed out on knowing how smart and good she is. You missed out on her beautiful smile. You missed out on loving her."

She didn't know if her words registered in his dying brain. She hoped so. Wanda's parents missed out on loving her, too. All they ever did was tell her how evil she was, make her pray for hours, and beat her for allowing the devil into her heart. They missed out on having her love them as she grew up. Just like this pathetic old man had, they took advantage of her, too.

He worshiped drugs and booze. If he really was Angela's father, he should have worshiped her. Just like Wanda's parents, he missed out on life.

Wanda's chest heaved with the excitement of watching him bleed out, with the satisfaction of getting even with someone who had done her wrong.

The thought occurred to her that he wasn't the only one.

CHAPTER 14

Wanda felt good after leaving Albert dead in his dump. In fact, she felt more than good, she felt invigorated. She had killed a man who had caused her a lot of trouble, a man who needed to be dead. Killed him with her own hands. She felt a deep sense of satisfaction at having rid herself of a problem.

When someone finally found his body and reported it to the police, they would naturally assume that he had been killed and robbed by another homeless wino. Happened all the time. No one would ever have a reason to suspect Wanda of the killing.

With the problem of Albert out of the way, she was looking forward to having dinner with Ricky once he finished work for the day. She idly contemplated what she could fix him for dinner, what he would like, what would make him happy. She wanted him to be happy with her.

As she drove through town she thought about how easy it had been to kill both troublesome people—Ricky's wife and Albert. Not only had it been easy, it had been deeply satisfying.

Wanda found herself absently driving home. Not home to her new home with Ricky, but home to where she'd grown up. She was disgusted by the neighborhood as she drove past her parents' house. Junk lay in yards. Why did people leave junk in their yards? The little house where she had grown up looked even smaller than she remembered.

There were people out sitting on porches and hanging out on the street, so she drove past and parked in an alley a block away.

There were other cars parked in the alley. No one would think anything of her faded, old hatchback. It fit right in.

She was going to have to tell Ricky to get her a new car.

Wanda grabbed her big handbag off the passenger seat as she got out of the car.

It was a short walk out of the alley where she'd parked and into the next one. Her parents' house was near the middle of the block. Tall, weathered wooden fences surrounded most of the places. At other yards, chain-link fences kept barking dogs in.

The weedy dirt backyard at her parents' house was surrounded by a dilapidated wooden fence. Her parents didn't have a dog, so she didn't know why they didn't keep their yard up. They said dogs were a distraction from the Lord's path. Lawns probably were as well.

Angela fished her keys out of her handbag. She knew her father had changed the locks on the front door. She smiled to discover he had been too cheap to change them on the back door.

She was in kind of a daze as she walked into the familiar, haunted house of her childhood nightmares. She stood in the kitchen for a time, taking it in, letting her rage build.

Her father was due home any moment, so she knew her mother would be in the living room waiting so they could say their evening prayers before dinner. Wanda stood by the back door, waiting, too, and wondering why she hadn't thought of this sooner.

She heard the front door and her parents' voices. Her mother mentioned some things they would need to get from the store. Her father complained about his pants getting torn on a truck fender. Her mother said she could sew them.

After they had been silent for a time, Wanda pulled the big .357 Magnum revolver out of her purse. It was beginning to feel good in her hands. It made her the equal of those who had always tormented her. It made her better than them.

She took a deep breath to settle her excitement. She wanted to soak it all in. She had gone over it in her head a thousand times. Today it was finally the day.

Gun in hand, she walked into the living room. Her parents were kneeling, as she knew they would be at this time of day, before their little shrine in the alcove with a statue of the Virgin Mary to one side. The paint on the old plaster statue had been worn off on the edges in some places and was chipped in others. The tip of the Virgin Mother's nose was missing.

On her way into the living room, Wanda plucked the fat throw pillow from her father's chair and pressed it against the barrel of the gun.

"I'm home," she announced.

Startled, her father turned. "How did you get here? I told you, you are corrupt and sinful and aren't welcome in this God-fearing house anymore!"

Wanda shot him in the face.

Just as Brad had told her, the .357 hollow-point went in like a nickel and came out like a sack of quarters. The back of his head exploded out all over the picture of Jesus and the cross beside it. The Virgin Mary got new red robes. Bloody bits dripped down the wall.

Her mother sprang to her feet in surprise and horror.

"Wanda!"

Wanda shot her in the center of the chest before she could start bitching at her.

Surprisingly, her mother didn't even take a step. She simply dropped straight down into a heap, her arms and legs at loony angles.

Wanda looked to make sure she was dead and then tossed the pillow back on her father's chair. It had worked fairly well at muffling the sound.

She was a bit surprised at how easy it had all been. A lifetime of wishing they were dead, and now, here they were, dead. She remembered his interminable lectures of "you reap what you sow." How true. She wondered why she hadn't done it sooner and saved herself a lot of grief.

Wanda took her father's wallet out of his pocket and removed all the cash. There wasn't enough money to be of any real consequence, but she wanted the police to think it was a home invasion and robbery. In this neighborhood it wouldn't be surprising. She tossed the wallet aside. She removed her mother's wedding ring to add to the robbery theme. She would throw it in a dumpster later.

After making it look like the living room had been tossed looking for valuables, she went upstairs to their bedroom and opened all the dresser drawers, pulling out clothes as she went to make it look like the bad guy had ransacked the place. Since the police wouldn't know what valuables her parents had, they wouldn't have any idea what might have been stolen.

After she finished methodically staging the home invasion, murder, and robbery, she left out the back door. The police would think the bad guy had gotten in through the unlocked door.

The dogs in the fenced yards were still barking. They barked as they followed her along inside their fences as she walked back to her car. She knew most of these dogs. They barked virtually non-stop and were always ignored by their owners.

No one seemed to have paid any attention to the gunshots, either. In this neighborhood gunfire wasn't all that uncommon. Since no one came out of their houses to look, Wanda guessed that being inside the house and using a pillow must have muffled the shots enough that no one took note.

Back in her car, she drove calmly away, exhilarated and overwhelmed with a sense of satisfaction.

She couldn't believe how easy it was to kill people and get away with it if you knew what you were doing.

CHAPTER 15

Wanda's parents didn't have any life insurance, and they didn't have bank accounts. Her father didn't believe in banks, so he kept what little cash he had in a tin box on the top shelf in the bedroom closet. Wanda had taken the cash and left the box on the floor with half the clothes in the closet. It amounted to a few hundred dollars. He always felt guilty for keeping some money for himself and not giving it to the church. No doubt he prayed for forgiveness, so he could be absolved of guilt and still have the money. He had always prayed after beating her, too, probably to be absolved of that as well.

It was several days before the bodies were discovered. The police called Wanda and asked her to come in. She cried and gasped in shock over the murders the whole time they asked questions. The police asked if she knew of anyone who could have had a beef with her parents. She told them that everyone loved her God-fearing parents. After exhausting their list of questions, the police thanked her for coming down and said they were sorry for her loss. Idiots.

Wanda didn't tell Ricky what had really happened. What would be the point? The less he knew, the better. All he knew was what she had told him about how badly they had treated her growing up and how her father had beaten her, so he wouldn't need to pretend he was sad.

Her parents had owed more on their house than it was worth, so the bank was going to take it. That was fine with Wanda. She didn't ever want to see the place again.

Since her parents had no life insurance, Ricky paid for the funeral. Wanda contributed most of the cash she had taken from their house. She said it was her savings from tips at the bar. He said it wasn't necessary, but she said they had been her parents and she wouldn't have it any other way. He nodded his understanding.

The service at the church went on forever, with a long sermon and then prayers for their souls. The funeral itself was simple, but nice. Her mother's casket was open, her father's closed. Their friends from church came and cried and prayed their little hearts out. They all told Wanda how sorry they were. She dabbed her eyes and thanked them.

The graveside service was mercifully short.

She was relieved when it was all over.

Life with Ricky gradually settled down to a routine. While he was busy at work earning money, she kept the house tidy and cooked dinner for him. The beautiful house came to feel homey. She was happy there.

But there was one thing still nagging at her, the same thing that had been bothering her for quite some time, the thing she couldn't get over.

She missed Angela in her life.

The more time that went by, the more important she realized Angela had been to her.

Even though she had Ricky and a wonderful house, she still felt empty inside. Life seemed flat. Angela was somehow bigger than life. Wanda missed Angela and wanted to be friends with her again, so she decided she would see if she could get back her old job at the bar.

It felt good driving into the parking lot at Barry's Place again. The good part of her old job was that people in the bar liked her. She'd had a lot of fun there. It had been where she'd met Ricky.

Being a weeknight it wasn't busy, so she was pretty sure she would have a chance to talk to Barry and ask for her job back, but first she really wanted to see Angela.

Wanda was relieved to see that Angela's primer-gray pickup was in the parking lot. Barry would be there as well. Barry was always there. Wanda planned on being giggly and coy when she asked Barry for forgiveness and her old job back. He was a softhearted guy, so she was pretty sure she could talk him into it. That way she would be working with Angela again. That way they would just naturally get back to being friends and spending time together at the bar.

It was a dream come true living with Ricky in such a nice house, but it would be the cherry on top to get back in Angela's good graces again. Wanda would make it up to her somehow. Maybe she could get Angela a puppy. She would be the best friend Angela had ever had.

Inside the bar, men recognized her and shouted their greetings. Wanda grinned and winked on her way past. It felt good. She didn't see Barry, but Angela was behind the bar.

Wanda walked up to the bar and hopped up on a stool right in front of Angela. She slung her big handbag up onto the next stool and then folded her arms on the bar as she leaned in.

When Wanda looked up into Angela's eyes, the world stopped.

Wanda's mouth went dry. Her fingers tingled. She felt hot and faint.

She sat paralyzed at the look on Angela's face, but mostly at the look in her eyes.

She knew.

It was crystal clear in her eyes. Angela knew. There wasn't a shred of doubt in Wanda's mind that Angela knew everything. Wanda didn't know how she knew, but she knew it all.

Wanda snatched up her handbag and ran out of the bar.

CHAPTER 16

Angela's phone rang as she walked out into the dimly lit parking lot. The call was from Wanda. She had known it would be. Angela could see her car across the parking lot, Wanda sitting in it, phone in hand.

She answered the call but didn't say anything.

"Angela?" Wanda asked after a moment of silence. "Angela? Are you there?"

Angela stopped where she was as she watched Wanda across the parking lot. "I'm here."

"Angela... I'm so sorry."

"What are you sorry for, Wanda?"

"I'm sorry that I shot your dog," she said in a tearful voice.

It took Angela a fraction of a second to realize what Wanda was talking about. When she had found the cigarette butt, Angela had suspected Albert. For some reason she had also suspected Wanda, because it had just seemed like somehow crazy Wanda would be involved. But it still surprised and saddened her to hear the confession.

"Why would you have done that, Wanda?"

Wanda was choking in tears, now. "It's a long story, but I thought you had told Ricky's wife about him and me."

"I didn't approve of what you were doing, and told you so, but I'm not a snitch."

"I know." Angela could see her nodding in her car. "I know. I was so stupid."

"You were stupid about a lot of things, Wanda."

"What do you mean?"

"They found the body of Ricky's wife today. The property owner noticed where a vehicle had stopped. He saw footprints. It made him curious, so he investigated and found the body."

Wanda was silent.

"You really blew it this time, Wanda."

"What do you mean?"

"The police arrested Ricky this afternoon. Now they're looking for you."

"You mean Ricky killed his wife?"

"Oh please, don't try to bullshit me, Wanda. I know what you did."

"You couldn't possibly know."

"I told you I was born a freak, remember?"

"Yes, but I don't know what that means."

"My mother used drugs. Lots of drugs. Because of that I was born broken. I don't feel things like normal people. But it also left me with the freaky ability to recognize killers just by looking in their eyes. And when I look into their eyes, I see more than their guilt. I see everything they've done. Everything. I see everything about those sins written on their soul.

"When I looked into your eyes a few minutes ago, I saw everything. I think you realized that, didn't you? That's why you ran out."

"But the police won't be able to—"

"The police aren't stupid. The forensics lab will look at the nylon cable tie from around her throat. They will find tool marks on the end of that nylon tie. They will go looking for the tool that left those marks.

"They will find a pair of pliers on the workbench in Ricky's garage."

"How could you possibly...?"

"The forensics lab will match the tool marks on those pliers to the marks on the cable tie from around the neck of Ricky's dead wife."

"So Ricky—"

"I told you, cut the BS. I already saw in your eyes that you ran and got those pliers because Ricky couldn't pull the cable tie tight enough around his wife's neck. The police will find your fingerprints on those pliers. They will inspect the rope you and Ricky wrapped around the body. The forensics lab will find some dark hairs tangled in that rope. DNA analysis will show those hairs to be from you."

"But my fingerprints on the pliers don't mean—"

"Your fingerprints are also on the knife you shoved through Albert's throat."

That gave her pause.

"Did you ever think to wipe off your fingerprints? Did that ever occur to you, Wanda? Didn't you think the police would check the murder weapon for prints?"

She stammered for a moment, trying to find her voice. "I...I thought they would assume it was another homeless drunk who killed him and robbed him. They were supposed to think it was another drunk."

Wanda sounded desperate, wanting it to be so. In a way, Angela felt sorry for her. She was a killer, and deserved to die, but Angela felt a little sad for how Wanda wasn't able to think things through and simply thought she could get away with things because she wanted to. But then, killers always thought they would get away with it. They never considered consequences. They never realized how smart the authorities were.

"Then you went to your parents' house," Angela said, "and you murdered them. You used a throw pillow from your father's chair to muffle the shots. The bullets will match the gun you stole from Brad. The gun you have in your big handbag."

"My parents were monsters!"

"Maybe so," Angela said, "but they never murdered anyone."

The cold logic of that left Wanda speechless. It often had in the past when Angela pointed out what should be obvious.

Wanda's car was parked near the streetlight. Angela could see her lean over and pull the revolver out of her handbag.

When she did, Angela switched her phone to her other hand and pulled her own gun out of the holster inside the waistband at the small of her back. Gun in hand, she started walking slowly, deliberately, toward Wanda's car.

"What's going to happen to me?" Wanda asked through tears.

"The police aren't stupid. You left evidence everywhere, Wanda. They've already arrested Ricky. Ricky never had much of a spine. He just did what you told him to do. He's going to start singing. Today, tomorrow, the next day, he will break down and confess everything. He will want to minimize his role, so he will say it was all your doing. To bolster his story, he will tell them how you spit in his wife's face while she was dying.

"The forensics lab will match DNA they find on her face to you. The police are going to find your fingerprints on the pliers just like they are going to find your prints on the knife you put through Albert's throat, just like they are going to find your fingerprints on your father's wallet that you tossed aside after you took out the cash."

Wanda hung her head as she cried silently for a moment.

"I made Albert suffer for what he did," she finally said. "For what he did to you. If Albert really was your father, he should have loved you like I do."

"You have a crazy way of showing love, Wanda."

"Not crazy to me."

"That's the problem," Angela said softly into her phone.

"Angela…what's going to happen to me?"

Angela didn't ever allow killers to get away with killing. It was her strange calling. It was what she lived for. It was her only reason for living. It was her purpose.

Although what she did with killers was justice, the police wouldn't see it that way, so she didn't ever want to be caught. For that reason, she never left bodies where they could be found.

In this case, though, Wanda had a gun in her hand, a gun she had used to murder her parents. Whether or not she pointed it at Angela didn't matter. It would be seen as self-defense, so this time there was no need to worry about the body.

Wanda's car was sitting at a slight angle. The window would deflect a small .22 round in an unpredictable way. Angela needed Wanda to roll down the window so she would have that clean shot. Then it would be over in an instant. Wanda wouldn't know what hit her. She would simply cease to exist.

Angela kept the gun hidden behind her thigh as she held the phone up to her ear with her other hand.

"Angela," Wanda cried over the phone, "I'm so scared. What's going to happen to me?"

"The truth? If you surrender, or run and are captured, you will be arrested, tried, and convicted of four murders. If they don't give you a death sentence, you will spend the rest of your life in a living hell, never to be free again.

"The thing is, Wanda, one way or another, you are going to pay for your sins. Sooner or later, one way or another, everyone pays for their sins."

As Angela got closer, she could finally see Wanda's eyes as she wept. "Crazy Wanda," she murmured to herself. Wanda always acted first and thought later.

"Come on, Wanda," Angela whispered, "roll down your window. It will all be over before you know what happened."

Wanda just sat there, gun in hand, phone to her ear.

"Angela..."

Angela stopped not far from the car.

"What?"

"Angela, I finally understand what that tattoo on your throat means. You said one time to pray that I never had reason to know what it meant. But now I know. You really are a dark angel. A dark angel sent for me."

As Angela watched, Wanda put gun the barrel in her mouth.

A sudden sound, like a sledgehammer wrapped with a T-shirt striking an anvil, rang through the still darkness.

The inside of the car windows instantly misted with red.

Angela stood staring for a moment, then slipped her gun back in the holster under her top at the small of her back.

This was one body of a killer she had no desire to see.

She turned and walked back to the bar. Her part in this was over. Wanda was no more.

Someone else would discover the body and call 911.

Angela didn't ever get involved with the authorities if she could avoid it. With this, she could avoid it. Soon, someone else would call them.

She didn't know if she would ever see Bardolph again, but if she did, she would tell him that his mate's killer was dead. Somehow, she thought he would understand.

Read more about Angela Constantine in the major novel

THE GIRL IN THE MOON

and in the novella

TROUBLE'S CHILD

Made in the USA
Lexington, KY
02 February 2019